KAY THOMPSON'S ELOISE

Eloise at the Ball Game

STORY BY **Lisa McClatchy**

ILLUSTRATED BY **Tammie Lyon**

Ready-to-Read

Simon Spotlight

New York   London   Toronto   Sydney   New Delhi

SIMON SPOTLIGHT
An imprint of Simon & Schuster Children's Publishing Division
1230 Avenue of the Americas, New York, NY 10020
Copyright © 2008 by the Estate of Kay Thompson
All rights reserved, including the right of reproduction in whole or in part in any form.
"Eloise" and related marks are trademarks of the Estate of Kay Thompson.
SIMON SPOTLIGHT, READY-TO-READ, and colophon are
registered trademarks of Simon & Schuster, Inc.
Designed by Christopher Grassi
The text of this book was set in Century Oldstyle.
Manufactured in the United States of America
First Simon Spotlight edition October 2011
First Aladdin Paperbacks edition March 2008
8 10 9
Library of Congress Control Number 2007939167
ISBN: 978-1-4169-5803-1
0715 LAK

My name is Eloise.
I am a city child.

"Please get dressed.
We must go!" Nanny begs.
"Coming, Nanny!" I say.

Weenie and I put on our
team shirts.
And our lucky hats.

We are going to a baseball game.

Our seats are
behind home plate.

"Popcorn here!" yells a boy.
"Popcorn here!" I yell.

Oh I love, love,
love popcorn.

"Hot dogs here!" yells a boy.
"Hot dogs here!" I yell.

Oh I love, love, love hot dogs.

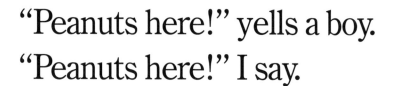
"Peanuts here!" yells a boy.
"Peanuts here!" I say.

Oh I love, love,
love peanuts.

"Cotton candy here!"
yells a boy.
"Cotton candy
    here . . . ," I say.

"No, no, no, Eloise!" Nanny says.
"Yes, yes, yes," I say.

"You look green, Eloise,"
    Nanny says.

"I feel green," I say.
"No more snacks, Eloise."

"Look at home plate!" Nanny says. "It is your favorite player!"

My favorite player is up at bat.
He hits the ball.

The ball flies right at us!
"Foul ball!" yells the umpire.

"Look out!" Nanny says.
"Look out!" a boy yells.

I take off my lucky hat.

I skibble to the left.

I skibble to the right.

I jump as high as I can!
I catch the ball!

"Great catch!" yells the boy.
"Well done!" says Nanny.
I do a victory dance.

I give Weenie a high five.
I kiss my lucky ball.

"Eloise," begs Nanny.
"Sit, sit, sit! Your player is
going to try again!"

Nanny and I hold hands.
The pitcher winds up and
throws the ball!
"Oh, no!" I yell.

"Oh, my!" says Nanny.
The ball goes right up
over our heads!
"Foul ball!" yells the umpire.

I try to send my player
my special signal.
"Keep your eye on
the ball!" I yell.

I cover my face.
It is hard to watch.
He hits the ball.
It is going, going, gone!

"Home run!" yells the boy.
"We won!" I yell.
"Well done," says Nanny.

The crowd roars!
Oh I love, love, love baseball.